Copyright 2012 Dennis Snyder
All rights reserved

This is a work of fiction. Names, characters, places and incidents are products of the author's imagination or are used fictitiously and any resemblance to actual events, locales or persons, living or dead, is entirely coincidental.

All rights reserved. No part of this book may be used or reproduced in any manner without written consent from the author.

Cover photo compliments of http://www.freedigitalphotos.net used with permission.

The second book of the Lake Haven Murder series is a work in progress. The book ***Golf Course Massacres*** will be released in mid November 2012. Leave your email at www.concerninglife.org and we will keep you up to date on the progress.

Other fiction work by Dennis Snyder:
Road Rage vs. Forgiveness A short story

Non-Fiction work by Dr. Dennis Snyder:
The Importance of Prayer

PERSONAL VENGEANCE

A Novella

Dennis Snyder

Concerning Life Publishing

Dedicated to my lovely wife Vicki

Chapter One

Pastor Mike McIntyre turned onto Jackson Street and swerved to avoid the emergency vehicles blocking the road. Parking his motorcycle, he headed over to a police officer attempting to control the gathering crowd. "Hi officer, I'm Pastor McIntyre from the Gospel Chapel. Can I offer any spiritual help?"

The police officer nodded and pointed "Go see Detective Oakes over there."

As Pastor Mike closed in on Detective Jim Oakes, he caught the stench of stale beer and smoke on his brown sport coat. Sticking out his hand, Mike quickly introduced himself to the clean shaved, sandy haired cop and asked if he could be of any service. It was obvious to Mike, from the once over he was given by the Detective, that he did not meet Oakes' idea of a pastor.

"What church did you say you were with?"

"The Gospel Chapel, over on First Street, right across from the elementary school. What happened?"

"Some lady backed into a parked motorcycle that belonged to a member of the Sons of Lucifer Motorcycle gang." After lighting his cigarette he continued, "Five of them got carried away and savagely beat her. We're not sure she's going to make it. The ambulance should be here any time. Could you go over and see what you can do for her?"

"No problem." said Mike

As he turned toward the scene, Detective Oakes grabbed his arm and said, "Her face is so severely beaten the nose is broken, teeth have been knocked out and her jaw is in pieces. She is not able to talk and it is a bloody mess. The five gang members fled taking her wallet with them and we haven't been able to identify her."

Pastor Mike removed his leather jacket before he knelt down to comfort and pray with the victim. It was hard to look at the woman's bloody and distorted face so he looked square in her eyes. As the beaten woman looked back, shivers ran up his back and terror struck his heart. Before Pastor Mike could get his composure the EMTs shoved him out of the way. Within minutes they had her loaded into the ambulance and was headed toward the hospital. Still in shock, he stared at the ambulance as it raced off. After what seemed like an eternity, reality sunk in when Detective Oakes handed the pastor's jacket to him and asked, "Were you able to give her any comfort?"

"That's my wife!" said Pastor Mike grabbing his jacket. "I need to get to the hospital."

Before Oakes could say anything, Pastor Mike was strapping on his helmet and mounting his bike. Racing to the hospital weaving in and out of traffic the pastor's mind also raced as he thought of life without his beautiful wife of fifteen years. He knew that they did not have the perfect marriage but it was close. They had worked hard to keep God first in their lives. They spent many hours counseling couples on what a biblical marriage was all about and they did their best to apply the Word of God in their own relationship. No way would God take Pam away yet! They still had years of life and ministry together.

Mike was familiar with the hospital having spent hours with others ministering to their needs. He rushed directly to the emergency room just behind the ambulance carrying the woman of his dreams. He stood to the side as the doctors and nurses attended to his wife. No one asked him to wait outside. He was a familiar face to most of these men and women who worked in the ER. They had seen him many times with moist eyes and a comforting arm around a loved one as he silently prayed for them. One nurse even remarked to the ER doctor, "It looks like Pastor Mike beat the family here."

The doctor seemed to ignore her as he placed his stethoscope on Pam's chest and yelled, "We need to get her to the operating room, stat!" The ER emptied quickly as they wheeled Pam into the elevator to the third floor leaving him standing alone. After a few minutes Mike turned and walked to the surgery waiting room. He informed the volunteer why he was there and that he would be down the hall in the hospital chapel.

"I'll call the hospital chaplain to meet you." the volunteer said.

Mike knew no one would come; he was the chaplain on call.

The blue green of the stained glass behind the cross shimmered from the dim light of candles burning on the table to the right of the altar. The four pews were empty amplifying the hollow sound of his footsteps in the chapel.

One hour earlier...

"Hi honey, how's work going?" Pam said.

"Hey Babe, it's going well, I almost have my Sunday outline ready and will be fleshing it out later today. How about your day?"

"Not so good. Mary lost the baby and I just left her house. It brought back a lot of memories that I need to address."

"I'll meet you in an hour Babe. How about lunch at JW's on Jackson Street? The rain has dried up and the sun is out so why don't I bring the bike? We can go for a good ride and cry after we eat."

"Ok Mike, but we will have to talk about the baby again."

"I know Babe; I will see you at noon. Love ya."

"I love you too. Bye," as Pam hung up the phone she felt her car back into something.

Mike kicked back in his chair as he wiped his tears. He and Pam had lost their only child in her second trimester over five years ago. Their hearts still ached with the loss and they could empathize with others. He knew that they would gain strength as they focused on God's Word and His promises. Pam's favorite place to pray was on the back of the Harley Fatboy with the wind in her face.

Back at the Chapel . . .

Pastor Mike knelt at the Altar. "Our Gracious, Heavenly Father, Almighty God, I am at a loss for words this time. It's Pam. She's in bad shape. She may not make it Lord, if you don't intervene." The pastor wept uncontrollably as he thought about losing his wife. "God, if you will spare her I will do anything you ask, I will go anywhere you want me to go. Just don't let her die. You know that she's my life. Where would I be without her? Lord, please I beg of you…"

Just then he felt a hand on his shoulder. Looking up he saw the doctor and the look in his eyes . . .

Chapter Two

"Dave, what time will the people start to get here?" asked Pastor Mike

Dave, a slight man in his mid fifties with a touch of gray in his otherwise coal black hair, was the only funeral director in the small Midwestern town of Lake Haven, KY. Lake Haven was a bedroom community about 40 minutes South West of Cincinnati.

"Why don't you try to relax a bit, Mike, you've been pacing for 20 minutes now. Take a seat with the rest of the family. The folks will start arriving in five minutes or so. It is going to be a long night and a tedious morning at the Chapel tomorrow."

"Dave, I've spent many hours in this very room comforting grieving folks, but I'm lost! It's like I'm living in a fog? You have been a good friend over the years. Please help me get through the next 24 hours," said Mike as he again glanced at his watch. "All these details are overwhelming me."

"Listen Mike, God will get you through this. Give yourself to Him. You know we are praying for you all. I love you, Pastor."

"Dave, I've used those same words hundreds of times. I never realized how empty they really are. I know they're real. I know you love me. I know that you hurt for me. But how is God going to get me through this? I miss her!" Mike rubbed his eyes with the tissue Dave had given to him.

"Hi Pastor Mike, I am sorry for your loss." Jim Green, the associate pastor at the Gospel Chapel, was one of the hundreds who had come for the evening visitation. Jim, a very unassuming man had a love for His Lord and Savior that far outweighed his small stature. "All the details have been worked out for the services tomorrow. We will be singing a few of Pam's favorites and Pastor Breckinridge will be preaching the message. If you can think of anything special you would like to see just let me know and we will work it out."

"Thanks Jim. Pam would want the Gospel clearly presented. Other than that my mind is pretty numb right now. I will probably be taking a few weeks off. Do you think you can cover the pulpit for me?"

"Take your time. You have trained the leadership well. We can handle it until you are ready to jump in the saddle again." After a few awkward minutes Jim said, "You know we're only a phone call away. If you need anything, please don't hesitate to ask."

Over and over again Mike could hear himself say, "Thank you for your prayers and concerns. They are very much appreciated." As the evening wore on, Mike found himself just going through the motions of greeting those offering their condolences. At one point he leaned over to the graying, sixty-ish, woman on his left and said, "Mom Adams, I sure am glad they have a guest book to sign. I would never remember all these people without it."

"I know honey. I'm amazed at the number of people who've come out to pay their respects," said

Sarah Adams. Pam's mother had done a fantastic job in raising her only daughter. As a single mother she made sure that Pam and her brother Bart never missed church. Pam clung to the things of the Lord and continued to grow in her faith. Not having a father figure Bart rebelled early and was out of the house before his 16th birthday. Pam heard from him once or twice a year. He traveled around a lot and no one knew how to get in touch with him. Bart would be in for a surprise the next time he called.

For the last 12 years Mike and Pam lived and ministered in Lake Haven. As Mike looked over the room, memories came flooding back of individuals that Pam's life had touched.

* * * * *

"6:30 already! I just closed my eyes. Hey Babe, time to get…" Mike slowly pulled the covers up to his neck as he began to weep.
"Lord, how am I going to get through this? What have You done to me? I have been faithful to You and You allowed this to happen! Why me! Why Pam! How could You!" Mike rolled over and wept uncontrollably before he got out of bed. After a strong cup of coffee he jumped in the shower, shaved and put on his favorite suit.

* * * * *

Dave was there to greet Pastor Mike as he entered the Chapel. "Hi Mike, how did you sleep last night?"

"How do you think I slept? It was a terrible night. I couldn't shut off my mind. What's on the agenda today?"

"Sarah and your mom put a good selection of pictures together. We will set a few of them up front where the casket usually is. From 10:00 to 11:00 the visitation will be here in the foyer. Somewhere around 10:45, the family will meet with Pastor Breckinridge for prayer in the conference room. At 11:00, the Pastor will lead you and the family in to be seated and the service will begin." Placing his hand on Mike's shoulder he asked in a soothing voice, "Does that sound okay with you?"

"Yeah, that's fine. Whatever, it really doesn't matter. I can't believe that they won't release her body. That ticks me off!"
"Mike, you know that with a murder case, they have to keep the body. They need to do an autopsy and keep the body for evidence. When they release her, we will have a grave side service."
"McIntyre!"
Mike looked over and saw the well dressed, graying, hulk of a man lumbering over to him. Bible in hand and a tear on his cheek.

"Pastor John! Thank you for coming to do this for me. Pam wouldn't want anyone else to officiate her funeral. You were like a father to her."

"We had some great times together, Mike. I sure wish the Lord had not moved you. You were the best associate I ever had. You and Pam sure touched a lot of lives in your four years at Calvary Bible."

Pastor Mike tried to listen as his friend and mentor shared his thoughts during the service. But he became oblivious to his surrounding as his mind went to happier times.

Five years earlier...

"Mike, Mike, I'm pregnant! We're having a baby," cried Pam excitably as she burst into his office

"Alright, it's about time," exclaimed Mike as he jumped to his feet and grabbed his lovely wife. "It seems like we've been trying all our lives. What did the doctor say? How far along are we? Is it a boy or girl? Come on spit it out. What did he . . ."

"Shut up long enough and I'll tell you! I'm two months along. Everything looks great. We need to get an ultrasound before we'll know if it is a boy or a girl. Are you sure you want to know?"

"No, I'm not sure. Maybe we should wait until he's born to find out."

"He? Sounds like you have your mind already made up, Dad."

"Aw, come on, Pam. You know it doesn't matter to me as long as he/she is healthy and . . ."

"Mike, the service is over. We need to go over to fellowship hall for lunch," said Joyce McIntyre. A tall, slender and attractive lady in her mid sixties took charge and walked with him to the luncheon. Following quietly behind, walking tall in his best suit was Ned. Mike's dad had been the silent leader in the home as long as Mike could remember. Mom's the vocal one, but dad runs the show.

"Pastor Mike, you go first. Your mom and dad and Sarah will follow. We'll have plenty of sandwiches and salads so take as much as you want."

"Thank you, Sally. You're a gem to have around."

Sally, looking younger than her years, even with her white hair, had been the funeral hospitality lady in the church for almost 37 years. She had the food laid out to perfection and made sure that no one would go away hungry.

"Ruth we're going to need more lunch meat for sandwiches. I can't believe how many people are here. I hope we can find room for them. Can you run to the store?"

"Sure, how much do we need?"

Chapter Three

"Oakes, some guy on line one asking for you," said the desk Sergeant sticking his head around the corner.

"Detective Oakes, what can I do for you?"

"Hi Detective, this is Mike McIntyre. I am calling about my wife's case and wondering if you've learned anything new?"

"Well, Pastor McIntyre, you know that it's only been a couple of weeks and we're making headway in the case. We have no doubt that five members of the Sons of Lucifer Motorcycle club murdered your wife, but we can't prove which five it was."

"I wouldn't call that group of motorcycle riders a club. It's more like a degenerate gang of murderers and thugs! You need to go arrest them all and force them to tell us who did this. They need to pay for what they've done!" Mike was oblivious to the pain as he hit the wall with his fist.

"Unfortunately it's not that simple Pastor. There are over fifty members and they all alibi each other. We can't make a case without some hard evidence and they left us none at the scene. We're doing the best we can. Lake Haven has the best investigators in the State."

"I know. I'm not blaming you but someone has to pay for the murder of my wife. These guys can't be that smart to not get caught. Come on they're just a bunch of hoodlums."

"I know how you feel. It'll just take us some time and we'll get these guys for something. They'll spend time in prison sooner or later. As you said they're not all that bright."

"I want these guys to pay for Pam's brutal murder not some stupid B&E. These guys deserve the chair. If the police can't do something maybe I can! I've gotta go Detective."

Mike paced the floor for hours, totally blocking from his mind and heart God's Word, "Vengeance is Mine, I will repay, says the Lord…Do not be overcome by evil, but overcome evil with good," as he thought about ways to get even with the five men who had shattered his life. In the last hours of the night, Pastor Mike knew each step that he would take to exact his own brand of personal vengeance on these men.

* * * * *

Pastor Mike strolled into the Chapel's office early the next morning and handed a letter to Pastor Jim Greene. Pastor Jim was a bit taken back as he peered at the unshaven, un-kept, worn out man in front of him. "What's this?"

"It is my letter of resignation. I'm leaving the pastorate, selling the house and moving on."

"Wait a minute! Don't make some sort of hasty decision give it some time. It has only been two weeks and . . . "

"I've made up my mind and no one is going to change it. I know what I need to do" said Mike, as he leaned on the edge of Jim's desk

"Pastor, have you talked with the Lord on this?"

"I don't need the Lord to tell me what to do. I'll be making my own decisions from now on. And I've made this one. I'm done in the ministry."

Pastor Jim was blown away by this uncharacteristic move by his senior pastor. This was a man who always went to the Word of God and prayer for all his decisions. Now he's making one of the biggest decisions of his life without the Lord's guidance.

"Pastor, do you realize what this will do to so many people you have taught and helped?"

"You know what Jim; I can't concern myself with everybody else. I need to do what I need to do and it doesn't include the ministry or God's people. In fact it doesn't even include God! This is on my own and nothing is going to stop me. Enough said, please pass the letter of resignation on to the board." Mike turned and walked out of the church without as much as a goodbye to anyone on the staff.

Before Jim could get out from behind his desk and out the door he heard the snarl of Pastor Mike's fatboy pulling out of the parking lot.

Over the course of the next couple days things were hot and furious at Pastor Mike's. Everything was up for sale. Furniture, lamps, cars, even his fishing boat was on the block, everything that was except the fatboy. The elders of the church came by trying to talk their pastor from stepping down. Mike and Pam's family tried to slow him from making unwise decisions. Some of his closest friends were in tears watching him walk away from his Lord. All to no avail. Mike's mind was made up.

Four weeks after Pam's murder, Mike had sold or given away everything, including the dog. The house was listed with a real estate agency. Mike packed a small leather bag and rode off, cutting all ties with his old life.

Chapter Four

"Hi, I'm Sam and welcome to Fast Eddies Sporting Goods" said the young man waiting at the door. "How may I help you sir?"

"Hi Sam, just call me Mac" said Pastor Mike "Can you direct me to the weight training stuff and a large punching bag?"

"It is right over here in our fitness corner. Is there something special you are looking for besides the punching bag?"

"I will need a weight bench, a weight set, including dumbbells, the punching bag and some gloves. You do deliver right?"

"If you buy all that stuff I can get it delivered for free within 25 miles."

"Great, show me what you have," he said as he threw a right punch into the bag hanging on display. "That felt good I'll take that, this bench and that set of weights."

"Ok" said Sam. "Let's see what size glove you need and which set of dumbbells would you like? This set here is adjustable and can go from 5lbs all the way to 30 lbs."

"Those will do it. Deliver them to this address. It is the abandoned West Side Auto Repair shop on 8th Street. I'll be there tomorrow between 8:00 AM till 5:00 PM. Here is my cell number if you need to get a hold of me for any reason."

"That'll be no problem, Mac. In fact, I'll try to have the delivery guys there by 9:00AM. I really appreciate your business."

As Mac left Fast Eddies he climbed aboard his Harley and 20 minutes later pulled into the small auto repair shop he had rented on the West side of Cincinnati. The business had closed abruptly after the new bypass was built. All the tools and equipment were left behind and was perfect for what Pastor Mike had in mind.

With no time to waste Mac grabbed the phone book and called the first listing for a personal Fight Trainer.

"All About Fighting, this is Josh, how can I help you?"

"Hi Josh. I am a 35 year old guy and I want to learn how to fight can you teach me?"

"Well, that will depend on what kind of shape you're in and what kind of fighting you want to do?"

"I'm in decent shape and I just bought some exercise equipment to get in better shape. I want to be able to hold my own in any kind of street fighting and you only have until March to get me ready for anything that might come my way. Can you manage that?"

"Let's see that gives us about six months so if you are committed to it on a daily basis I am sure I can get you ready for what would come your way. Can I ask you why?

"You can ask but don't expect an answer. Just teach me how to fight!"

"Ok. Since I'm a personal trainer do you want to do this at my place or yours?

"Let's do it at mine. It is the old West Side Auto Repair shop on 8th Street. Can we start tomorrow at 1:00?"

"I don't see why not. It's $50 an hour and count on an hour or two a day minimum."

"No sweat I'll see you then at 1:00 tomorrow."

As Mac hung up the phone he glanced around the old place to see what he needed to do to get it ready for the fitness equipment and fight training. The place was pretty much the same as when the previous owner closed up shop two years earlier. A lot more dust and they did not pick up before they locked the door so there was much to be done.

The first service bay with the hoist would be perfect for rebuilding the fatboy. The far left corner would accommodate the fitness equipment with the front part for fight training. As Mac opened the door to the back room he found a small single bed, a dorm sized fridge, a microwave and a coffee pot making up the perfect sleeping arrangement for a single man with one thing on his mind. Yanking back the sheets on the bed Mac knew instantly that he would have to run up the street. Fortunately everything left in the fridge was unopened and the smell was limited to age.

An hour and a half later the new sheets on the bed, Ramen noodles on the shelf and a pot of coffee perking, the task of clearing out the area for the fitness equipment began. Most everything in that back corner was junk and the old dumpster in the back was full in no time as Mac cleaned. He dropped into the sack in the early morning hours worn out from using muscles he had not used in years as a pastor and was grateful that he fell asleep without dwelling on Pam's murder for the first time since it happened a little over a month ago

Startled by the banging on the front door Mac jumped out of bed to find the delivery men from Fast Eddies impatiently waiting to drop off his new fitness equipment. He flung open the service bay overhead door pointed and said, "Set it up over in the far left corner in that cleared out area."

"No problem, sir. But all we do is deliver you'll have to put every thing together yourself." said the older man.

Ok, I can do that. It can't be too hard and I do have the tools laying around here somewhere."

"There you go Mr. McIntyre, I just need you to sign here and we'll get out of your hair."

An hour later the punching bag was hanging from an upper beam, the weight bench was put together with the weights resting on the holder and Mac was eating some Ramen noodles and sipping coffee for breakfast. As he finished his coffee Mac began rifling through the front desk looking for a pen and paper to lay out his exercise plan. The lower left drawer was locked so he grabbed a large screwdriver and pried it open. Reaching in he pulled out a snub nosed 38 and a 45 automatic hand gun. Looking in the drawer he found cartridges for both guns. He opened the cylinder on the 38 loaded the gun and aimed it an old racing trophy on a shelf and pretended to pull the trigger as he mouthed "pow, pow" thinking how these guns will come in handy as he got his revenge on the Sons of Lucifer.

Chapter Five

"Hi, BadBoyz Piercing and Tattoos how can we ink you.

"Hey, I want to get a couple of tats what's a good time to come in?"

"Just about any time today would be good."

"If I come in around 11:00 can you be done before 1:00?"

"That will depend on what you want done. Why not come on in and see what we've got?"

"Ok, I will be there in 20" said Mac.

The roar of the fatboy filled the air as Mac sped off heading to BadBoyz for the first of many tattoos. Since the loss of Pam, Pastor Mike lost all abandon for safety when he rode the bike. Forget the helmet and speed laws were a thing of the past as he wove in and out of traffic passing on the right and the left was no big deal. He arrived at the tattoo parlor in 15 minutes and strolled in with bare arms looking for a couple of tribal tats.

"I think this one will do as an armband on my left and I like this larger one for my right from the base of the neck down through the forearm."

Susie, the leading tattoo artist at BadBoyz, said, "Great choice these will look good on your buff arms. We can do the smaller left one in about an hour and a half because it is all black but this larger one will take about three sittings so at least five hours for it."

"Sounds good to me, get started on the left arm, I have a meeting to be at by 1:00 this afternoon.

While you are at it why don't you pierce both ears too."

"Wow, you are really changing your look. What major thing has happened in your life to cause this?"

"Listen Susie Q, I don't need a therapist I need the tats. So less talking and more inking please."

"Ok, Ok, sorry I asked. Just trying to make conversation." said Susie as she swabbed Mac's left arm with alcohol "This won't hurt as much as the piercing will but you will feel some sharp pricks as we add the ink."

* * * * *

"Great job Susie and I'm sorry I was so short with you earlier. You were right the ear piercing hurt more than the tat did. When can I come back to get started on this arm?"

"How about tomorrow morning. We can get the whole thing outlined in about 2 hours. Let's say about 9 AM."

"Can we make it 8 instead and get it over with early?" Said Mac.

"I will see you in the morning at 8:00. That will be $65.00 for today's artwork and $15 bucks for the earring studs." Said Susie.

* * * * *

Josh Ward, from All About Fighting, was just getting into his pick-up when Mac rode up five minutes after 1:00.

Josh was a fairly muscular man in his late twenties with a crooked nose and a couple of noticeable scars on his face. He hosted a flat top marine style hair cut and had a bull dog tat on his upper arm with semper fi written underneath. He looked tough and it was obvious that he had been in a scrape or two in his short life.

"I'm Josh," he said as he shook Mac's hand. you didn't tell me your name yesterday on the phone, but my time is valuable to me if you are not going to be here on time you can find another fighter."

"I'm sorry Josh, my name is Mac, and I got behind some crazy old lady who wouldn't let me get around her. Sorry I cut it so close, it won't happen again. I've always been a stickler for being on time. Come on in."

As they walked in the front door Josh immediately scanned the entire building trying to get a feel for this stranger who had to be taught street fighting. The only thing that stood out was the section that was set up for training. Everything else simply looked like an old auto repair shop nothing out of the ordinary.

"I assume that we'll be using this area over here for training, right?

"Yeah, that was my thought. Will it work out?"

"No sweat. I think it might be good to get some floor mats down though. Once we start grappling we'll both be on the floor quite often. No sense getting hurt during training I figure whatever you have planned will hurt enough."

"Ok, I can pick some up. Any ideas where I can get some?"

"Actually, Mac, I have some extra at my place. I'll throw them into my truck when I come tomorrow."

"Great. About our training time can we move it up to say 8:00 AM? I have an appointment tomorrow but after that I'd like to get done with this early in the day. So tomorrow at 1:00 the rest of the time at 8:00. Will that work out for you?"

"That will work much better for me. You want to work out every day?"

"Seven days a week works for me. One day is like any other."

Josh thought for just a second before he answered, "I'm sorry but I attend church on Sundays and take that day off from fighting. But Monday through Saturday will be good. You'll need the break anyway. I'll be working you hard."

"You don't look like a church goer to me. Obviously you were a Marine and most likely saw a bunch of heartache. What took you to church?"

"My dad was a pastor before he died. I was raised in the church. Strayed away from the Lord while in the service. Now out of respect for my dad I continue to attend his old church with my mom. I don't believe much of it but it makes my mom happy. I attend and have dinner with her on Sundays."

"Well, that tells me you have a big heart, I sure hope you can teach me how to fight in spite of your church going. Just make sure you keep God out of the conversations."

"You can bet your friggin behind I can. I got a feeling we aren't going to get along to good. It'll be fun to kick your butt on a daily basis. Hit the bag and show me what you've got old man."

Seven in the morning came with not only muscle pain from fight training but continual soreness from the fresh tat of the day before. Mac threw on a pot of coffee and washed up as he prepared to head off to BadBoyz for the outlining of his right arm tattoo.

Shortly before he had to head out Mac sat on the desk top staring out the front windows. Pam's beautiful smile flashed through his mind as he remembered her invigorating personality. The joy that enveloped her face as she served the Lord was contagious. The sound of the phone shattered the stillness of the morning.

"Hello, this is Mac."

"Umm, hello, I'm trying to reach Pastor Mike McIntyre. Maybe I dialed the wrong number."

"No, you have the right number but I go by Mac now. Who's this?"

"Ok Pastor Mike. This is Sally and we have an offer on your house can we meet today to discuss it?"

"Oh hi Sally, like I said, I go by Mac now I'm no longer yours or anybody else's pastor. I can meet with you late this afternoon around 4:00, your office alright?"

Taken back by his rudeness sally paused, "Umm, yes, my office is fine. The offer looks pretty good especially in this economy."

"Ok then Sally, I will see you at four. I really do not care what the offer is I just want to unload the place. Bye."

Time had gotten away from him as he jumped on the bike a sped away realizing he would be late for his appointment with Susie.

"Susie, I'm sorry for being late it seems to be a common thing for me lately."

"No problem, sit down and we will get this monster tat outlined for you. How are your ears feeling?"

Chapter Six

"Can I help you sir?"

"Hi Sally, I am here about the offer on my house."

Startled by the appearance of the former man of God, her one time pastor, Sally let out an audible gasp as she looked at a total stranger. Round rings in his ears, tattoos the full length of his right arm and upper left arm, his hair noticeably longer and a full beard with tired blank eyes staring back at her.

"I'm sorry Pastor Mike, I mean Mac, I didn't recognize you"

"I understand I've changed a bit," he chuckled. "Show me what you have for an offer."

"I asked the prospective buyers to join us this afternoon. Here they come now. You might remember them they had just started to attend the church before Pam was murd...passed away."

"Sam and Beth Harvey you remember Pastor Mike McIntyre" Said Sally.

"Umm, yes hello Pastor Mike. How have you been," asked Sam, quite startled at Mac's appearance.

"I've been better but please call me Mac, I'm no longer a pastor just a regular guy now. So you want to buy my house. Sold! Fill out the paper work Sally and give me a call when it is time for the closing."

"Mac you haven't even heard the offer."

"They need a house and I need to sell. Get the paper work ready and give me a call. I've gotta go. I can't handle this B.S. It brings back to many memories." The others were shocked at his rude behavior as he stormed out the door.

Mac headed out to the back roads to ride the curves and hills of Northern Kentucky in order to clear his head. After about an hour he pulled into a bar and grill on the outskirts of Fort Michell, KY.

"Give me a cheese burger, fries and a bottle of Bud."

Once his eyes adjusted to the dark room he noticed a number of bikers raising a small ruckus at one of the tables. They were not from the Sons of Lucifer but he watched them closely to see how an outlaw biker would act in public. What he saw sickened him. Lewd and crude as three of the bikers were hassling the waitress.

"Why don't you guys leave the poor girl alone? She's just trying to do her job." Said Mac.

"Who the hell do ya think you are buddy? You want a little piece of this action?" loudest of the three said. "Mind your own business or you will be eating my fist instead of that burger!"

"Ouch! Hands off my behind mister."

At that Mac jumped off his bar stool and landed a right punch on the big guys left check knocking him to the grungy floor. The other two jumped Mac and had him in their clenches as the loudmouth got up and wailed into the former pastor. Bloodied and bruised they tossed him out the front door.

"We don't want to see your face around this neck of the woods again! Next time will be the last time dude."

What have I gotten myself into. Have I bitten off more than I can handle? Can I become as bad as these guys? Will I be able to act this part or will it overtake me and destroy me? I need to get these guys for killing Pam. They don't deserve any mercy or grace. They deserve to die. I can do this I know I can. I'll learn to fight to the death if necessary. I will find those five guys if it's a last thing I do.

He reached into his saddlebag and pulled out the snub nose 38. Walking back into the bar and grill he grabbed the loudmouth bully by the hair, shoved the 38 into his temple. And said, "You messed with the wrong guy this time. Down on your knees! The rest of you keep your hands where I can see them or I blow this idiots head off. Now apologize to the lady and mean every word of it!"

"Ok man, don't get so worked up. Careful with that trigger finger! Sorry lady that we messed with ya."

"Not good enough buddy! I said like you mean it and do it politely"

"Ma'am, My boys and I are very sorry that we treated you in such an ugly way. We'll not let it happen again."

"That's better, Mac said. "Now get up and walk slowly with me to the front door. The rest of you stay put or your guy here gets a hole in his head."

"Dude, I don't know who you are but you're gonna to be sorry when I get my hands on you!" said the loudmouth.

"I don't figure on letting you get your hands on me. I'm going out this door now. Any of you sticks their head out before I'm long gone gets it blown off."

A quick, hard rap to the back of loudmouth's head and Mac was out the door and jumping on his ride before the outlaw bikers could get their thoughts together. The bikers got out of the door just as Mac pulled out of the parking lot. Jumping on their bikes they found that they could not get them started.

"My plug wire is gone" yelled the loudmouth, "Mine too"

"So is mine" yelled the third.

* * * * *

As Mac walked into the auto shop he gave his punching bag a good kick. Putting on his gloves he began a little practice with the bag. Bam, Bam, bang, whack and 20 minutes later with sweat rolling down his face Mac crashed in the front desk chair nursing his bruised ribs.

Chapter 7

As Mac pulled in to the used car lot a salesman met him as he put his kickstand down. A shady looking guy. Hair slicked back, sports coat and no tie, big rings and a gold chain around his neck. Definitely fit the stereotype for a used car dealer. "How can I help you sir? Looking to trade in that great looking bike?"

"Not on your life buddy." said Mac. "But I am looking for an old pickup truck. Don't need anything new just enough to get me through the winter. What do you have?"

"How much do you want to spend?"

"Any old truck will do. Don't want to spend much at all. Something cheap but reliable."

"Okay, I have an old Chevy half ton for a couple grand. Has decent tires, automatic, eight cylinder very little rust and runs like a top."

"Well let me see it."

"Okay let me grab the keys and we'll take it for a spin."

After a short ride around a couple of blocks Mac said, "It seems to run okay and sounds good. Can't say much about the looks. I'll give you $1500 for it."

"I don't know I'm really looking to get $2000. $1500 is a little low for this quality truck.

"Here's $1500 cash! Take it or I'm outta here."

"Okay, that'll work but you'll have to pay the taxes and the registration on top of the $1500.

"I figured that. Let's get the paperwork done so I can get out of here. I need it delivered to the old auto service garage on 8th street can you do that?"

"Sure what time you want us to drop it off?"

"How does nine-thirty tomorrow morning sound?" Mac said.

"We will be there with bells on." said the used car salesman.

* * * * *

Once back at the shop Mac began going through some of his American Iron magazines looking for anything with skulls and crossbones that he could put on the bike. He knew that now was the time to tear down the Fatboy and change the look from its rare yellow and black to a more custom outlaw looking ride. He knew that those idiots from the bar and grill would keep their eyes open for his bumble bee that rode out of the parking lot while they stood helplessly yelling profanity at him.

Jumping on the computer Mac ordered the parts he needed to make the drastic change on his ride. Pam hated to see skulls and crossbones and was always careful when she bought any kind of Harley shirts or sweatshirts for her husband so that they didn't send the wrong message to people they met as they rode. As Mac reflected back, her words haunted him. "I really like the style of this shirt. It'd look great on you. I wish they made it without the skull though." She said as she put the shirt back on the rack. "Try this one on. It won't look as good but it'll send a better message for the love of Christ."

"I'm sorry Pam but if I am going to fit in with these bikers I will need to look the part and so will the bike. I know you wouldn't have liked it but I need to get these guys for taking you away from me," Mac thought out loud.

Wiping away the tears, Mac headed to the service bay that needed to be cleaned up before he could begin tearing the sheet metal off of the bike. Standing with his hands on his hips staring at the mess his mind wondered off to a message he had preached about the end times.

"When the Lord comes back for His own there will be chaos in the world." Pastor Mike preached. "So many things will be left undone. Cooking pots will boil over, cars will be careening out of control. Airplanes will crash and thousands of lives will be lost because the pilots were taken away as the trumpet of God sounds."

There in front of Mac were tools left on the ground like the mechanic was working on a car when the rapture came. Even the pneumatic wrench was still connected to the air hose where a front tire would have been if the car were still on the hoist. He threw the tools into the rolling tool box. Glancing down at his right arm as he swept the floor he saw the incomplete tattoo and angrily said, "Doggone it, I forgot to call Susie to get this thing finished."

"Hi, BadBoyz Piercing and Tattoos, this is Susie. How can we ink you?"

"Hi Susie, this is Mac and I have half a tat on my arm. When can I come in and get some more work done on it?"

"Hey Mac, I was wondering when you were gonna come in. I've got some time right now if you can get away. We should be able to get an hour or so of color into it."

"Great, give me 15 to 20 minutes and I'll be there. I need to get this thing done."

Chapter Eight

Sitting on the front desk sipping his last cup of coffee Mac watched Josh as he got out of his truck walking with confidence coming through the front door.

"Morning, Mac, ready for some training," asked Josh as he threw his sport bag down and looked up at Mac. "Whoa, whose fist did you run into? Your face looks like it's been pummeled."

"Yeah, I ran into some guys that didn't like my correcting them. It was three on one and as you see I lost. That is one of the reasons I hired you, dude. Let's get to fighting. I've got someone coming at 9:30."

"Okay, let's do it. Have you been doing the daily exercises that I set up for you?"

"Sure and I've got to say you didn't make it easy. These are a tough work-out."

"Well, Mac they'll pay off in the long run. Let's start with some grappling moves so if you get ganged up on again you can break free from their grip." Josh said with a little chuckle.

"Go ahead and laugh but I held my own for a split second. Especially, since I've only been in training for less than a week. I've never been in a fight in my life until yesterday. I don't plan on losing another one."

"Listen Mac, I realize that you've been through something traumatic and you're making a bunch of changes in your life but it'd be easier to train you if I knew what you had planned."

"I appreciate that Josh, but all you need to know is that I want to be trained to kick butt without getting mine kicked too often. So let's get on with it." Mac said impatiently.

At that remark Josh grabbed Mac by the legs and threw him down. The fight was on as they wrestled around the mats until Mac was pinned and slapped the back of his opponent giving up.

"Okay, Mac, here is why I had it so easy in pinning you." Josh continued to show Mac some of the moves he had used to win so handily. Both men were winded after about an hour of defensive boxing training and grappling.

"Well, Mac, tomorrow is Sunday so I won't be in for training." Said Josh as he gulped a drink of cold water.

"That's right I get a day off. I think I'll need the break to mend my broken body. What church did you say you attended?"

"I don't think I told you. It's the Lighthouse Bible Church up in Fort Mitchell. It's pretty small so you probably never heard of it."

"Isn't Jerry Hurgt the pastor? Said Mac.

"You know Pastor Jerry?

"I have met him a couple of times at some meetings I used to attend. He seems like he knows what he is doing when it comes to the Word of God. Nice guy."

"What do you know about the Bible? I thought you told me to keep God out of our conversations"

"Hey, Josh, I have been around the block a few times. I wasn't always a grease ball looking for a fight. Here is your first check. Five hours training so that comes to $250. Correct."

"Yep, that will do it Mister McIntyre." said Josh as he glanced at Mac's real name on the check.

"Mister McIntyre is my dad's name you call me Mac and nothing else, got it?"

"Okay, Okay, don't get so hot under the collar. I'll see you at eight Monday morning. Unless you decide to stop by church tomorrow." Josh said as he walked out the door.

* * * * *

Josh helped his mother get seated toward the front of the church. Then he went looking for Pastor Jerry. "Pastor, I have a question for you."

"I hope it is a short one, morning worship starts in five." Reverend Jerry Hurgt had been the pastor at Lighthouse since Josh's dad died from a massive heart attack in the middle of his last sermon. Josh was always glad his dad died doing what he loved.

"It is. Do you know a Mike McIntyre?"

"Why, yes I do. Don't you remember a couple of months ago his wife was beaten to death by a bunch of bikers in downtown Lake Haven. He was the pastor over at The Gospel Chapel. He's a great guy and loves the Lord. I think he resigned after his wife died. He was the president of our IFCA Fellowship Sectional. I don't know what happened to him. Why do you ask?"

"I just saw the name yesterday and wondered if you had heard of him. Nothing important. Hey you better get up there it's time to start."

As Josh sat down next to his mother he couldn't help but think. *I wonder what this guy is up to? Why does a former pastor need to know how to fight? Why would someone who loves the Lord change so drastically? What have I gotten myself into?*

"Honey, we are all standing for the singing." said Josh's mom bringing him back to the moment.

Chapter Nine

When Josh walked into the old 8th street garage he noticed the now pony-tailed ex-pastor putting the finishing touches on the fatboy.

"Wow! What a difference. I think I liked the bumble bee look better than all this black skull and crossbones look. That bike has changed as much as you have over the last three months."

"Hey, Josh, how's it going for you this fine Saturday morning? I'm glad it is finally back together and it looks like warm weather tomorrow. Just right for a ride."

"I'm doing good. If the weather's good ride over and join us for church in the morning. Pastor Jerry would love to see you.

"You didn't tell him you knew me did you?" said Mac a little taken back from the remark.

"No don't worry. No one knows what you're doing. Whatever that is. Just thought I would invite you."

"Don't count on it. I haven't been in church for quite some time and don't really plan on it. Give me an update on how I'm doing as far as my fighting is concerned. I feel pretty confident if I say so myself."

"You have come a long ways that's for sure. You could probably hold your own with some of the best. You're a quick learner. However, you've not arrived quite yet. I've got more to teach you. When you can kick my butt, or at least give me a good fight, you'll be ready."

* * * * * *

Bam, brmm, brmm, rap, rap, rap. "Wow, is that loud without the baffles. I think I like it" Mac said to himself. "Time for a nice ride on this mean looking machine." Mac headed out toward the hills of Fort Mitchell. The late morning sun felt good on his neck as his hair whipped in the wind. Before he knew it Mac was overlooking the Lighthouse Bible Church nestled in the valley below. As he watched the people get out of their cars heading into the small brick building he wondered out loud, "I don't know if I can set foot in a church again. Why God, did you take the love of my life away from me? Why such a brutal death? What did we do to you that was so bad that we deserved this?"

Down below Josh caught a glimpse of Mac sitting on his ride but pretended not to notice as he walked into the church with a slight smile.

Mac wiped his cheeks as he started the bike and rode off into the country side surrounding Cincinnati.

* * * * *

After clearing his head with a three hour ride Mac pulled into a small family diner. Leaving with his belly full, Mac noticed a confrontation across the street near a small bar. Slowly moving to get a better view he saw that the three bikers he had a run in with at the bar and grill were hassling a lone man. Not liking the odds Mac walked over and calmly asked. "Anything I can do to help here?"

"Get out of here or I'll kick your butt." said the loudmouth as he turned to look at the stranger who dared to intervene. "Well looky here, now we've two to get rid of. It's the joker who put a gun to my head."

"I think the odds have changed. It's two against three instead of three on one. You three idiots don't have a chance against us. What's your name buddy?"

"I'm Billy. And you're right these guys are light weight for us. The problem is the other 15 in the bar. So we better make quick work of these guys and beat it out of here"

Mac was impressed with the way Billy handled himself as they put the three bikers down in a matter of seconds. Just then the door to the bar opened and their buddies started to pour out.

"My bikes across the street. Come on." Mac yelled.

"So's mine. See ya up the road dude."

Mac jumped on the fatboy and was on his way out when he saw Billy on his bike. He was cornered with no way out. He pulled out his 38 and came riding through the bikers shooting one in the leg as they sped off together. No one followed them.

"Billy pulled alongside Mac and yelled over their machines"Follow me I'll buy you a beer."

Chapter Ten

Mac followed Billy to the East side of Cincinnati. Pulling in front of a large building Mac read the sign hanging over the door, The Sons of Lucifer. His eyes widened as they parked their bikes in line with about 30 other machines.

What have I stumbled into? thought Mac. *Who was this guy he fought with just moments ago? How would the 'gang' deal with him being in their clubhouse?*

"Hey Billy, I'm not sure I should go in here? These guys don't know me and I don't need any more trouble than what I've got."

"Don't worry about it. I'm the VP of the club no one'll mess with you as long as you're with me. I didn't catch your name back at the ruckus."

"Name's Mac. If you're the VP why aren't you wearing your colors? I thought you guys never went anywhere without them?"

"I had to do some banking and that's easier without the colors. We're smarter than we make ourselves out to be," chuckled Billy. "Come on in and if anyone gives you any trouble tell them you're with me."

Once inside the clubhouse, if that's what they called it, Mac saw close to 40 men and women most with a beer in their hands. Surprisingly, the place was well lit and very clean and orderly. A long bar filled the North wall with more than a few bellying up to it. To the right of the bar stood a couple of pool tables. To the left a door with a neatly printed conference room sign hanging over it. The whole place quieted down when Billy and Mac walked through the door.

"What are you bringing him in here for?" said the largest, meanest and ugliest man Mac had ever seen.

"Hey Bubba, I figured it would be you to complain." said Billy as he climbed on top of a table.

Billy was just the opposite of Bubba. Good looking, mid-length brown hair with a wisp of a curl. As he mounted the table it was obvious that he had a confidence that most people only dream of having. His blue jeans and leather Harley jacket fit like they were made specifically for him.

Raising his hands he called out to everyone in the building. "Listen up Sons. Take a good look at this guy. Mac, get up here. His name is Mac and you WILL treat him with respect. He just saved my hide. The first one to give him any guff will answer to me. You all got that?"

"Yeah, we got it." roared the crowd.

"I don't like it Billy. You know the rules. In fact you wrote them. No one but members and pledges allowed in the hall. He's neither," crowed Bubba.

"I wrote the rules and I'm breaking them just this once. This is a special case, man. I'll tell you all the story after I've talked with Sonny. In the mean time don't mess with him, Bubba. If you do you'll be the one that's sorry."

Jumping down from the table Billy escorted Mac over to the bar. "Willie, give my man a beer on me and keep him company while I go in and talk with Sonny."

Willie unscrewed the cap off of a bottle of bud and set it in front of Mac. "Here you go handsome."

Willie, looked pretty handsome herself. She filled out her leather vest nicely and her long black hair wrapped over her shoulders both front and back. Her black eyes peered onto Mac's light blue ones with a twinkle that caught him off guard.

"Thanks. You been working here long?"

"I don't work here. Billy's my man. I sort of take care of the bar and make sure everyone keeps their tab short."

"You and Billy been together long?"

"About eight years. We met in college and been together ever since. I'm not sure I knew what I was getting into but I love the man. He got his MBA before I even knew he was part of the Sons. He and Sonny run this club like a welled oiled business."

Just then Bubba walked over and gave Mac a rough nudge pushing him away from the bar.

* * * * *

Sonny was sitting at the head of the conference table with glasses resting on the end of his nose. Sprawled in front of the burly man in his early 50s were a half dozen excel papers. Billy always got a kick out of Sonny's long flowing and thinning gray hair. It appeared to be out of place on a man of his age. Billy was smart enough not to make any comments about it. After all Sonny had been the leader of the Sons of Lucifer for over 15 years and held a lot of respect for his position.

"Hi Billy. You get that banking done? It took you long enough."

"Banking's all done. I did run into some trouble as I was leaving the bank"

"What happened?" said Sonny taking off his glasses and sitting up.

"Three of those idiots from the Fire Gang Club up in Fort Mitchell jumped me when I came out of the bank. I'm pretty sure they were planning on doing a little bit more than just a beating. If some guy hadn't got involved I would be toast right now."

"What happened to the guy?'

"I brought him back with me. He's out in the hall having a beer."

"You brought him here! What do you know about him? How do you know he's not a set-up."

"Relax, I wouldn't bring someone back here if I wasn't sure it was safe. He helped me wail on those dudes. When we left the rest of the gang had me cornered and Mac rode through them and shot one of them. Cops don't do that kind of thing."

"Billy. Bubba's giving your buddy a hard time out here." said one of the Sons sticking his head in the room.

Once the door was open they heard the ruckus plain as day.

"Okay Bubba, I don't want any trouble here. I just came because of Billy's invite. Just back-off man." said Mac.

"BUBBA, I said to leave him alone or you answer to me."

"Billy, I don't like this guy. What do you know about him?"

"I know he can whip your butt."

"If he's so tough, let me take him on in the cage. Nobody's beat me yet."

"How about it Mac? Want to take on this beast. It's a one on one in a locked cage. No holds barred and just short of death. Usually a broken bone or two." said Billy.

"I only wanted a beer not this."

"I guess he's not as tough as you think Billy."

"Keep your tights on Bubba. I didn't say I wouldn't do it. Where's the cage?"

"TIGHTS! I'm going to tear you apart sucker."

"Come on. The cage is in the back. This ought to be interesting. I've seen you both fight and the styles are definitely different." said Billy.

Chapter Eleven

Mac was amazed as he walked through the back door into a cavernous gymnasium style room. Right smack in the middle sat a professionally built fight cage surrounded by bleacher style seating. A microphone hung down from the ceiling in the center of the cage. Video cameras sat in each of the four corners with only one door into the cage. A basketball hoop hung in the far corner of the gym but appeared to be an after thought to the impressive fight scene.

"Wow." exclaimed Mac. "That's quite a sight. You guys take your fights too seriously."

"Yeah, the henchmen like to fight so we give em an opportunity with some control. Bubba's the champion. He's never been beat in the cage." said Billy.

"You've not beat him?"

"I've never fought him. Only the henchmen fight. The six of us who sit on the board are the elite. We might bet on a fight but we don't fight. At least not in the cage."

"Okay, so that makes me a henchman?"

"No. Only Sons are henchmen." Billy said sticking his finger in Mac's face. "You're not a Son and that makes you a nobody. Don't ever forget it. You're here because you helped me out of a sticky situation. I like you, but Bubba's family."

"Sorry, I didn't know. Does this mean that when I beat Bubba I'll have his whole family to deal with?"

"Not as long as you're fighting in the cage. If you were to beat him on the street you would be hunted. That's what's going to happen to those idiots we tangled with earlier. They will be put on our radar and picked off one by one. The Fire Gang is gonna bite the dust."

"Are you saying that they aren't as bad as you guys are."

"Ha, I am saying that there's nobody as bad as we are. Come on let's get you ready for your fight. Strip off that leather and throw on these shorts. I'll find you a pair of fight gloves and get you wrapped up."

Mac took off his jacket and tee shirt, dropped his jeans and put on the shorts. "You wouldn't happen to have a cup would you?" asked Mac.

"Nope. Cups aren't allowed anyways. None of the fighters wear them. Remember this is no holds barred. You can hit and kick below the belt. The only goal you have is to win with the fewest injuries. Let's get those hands wrapped up tight."

"Okay you heathens listen up." said the small but mouthy man in the middle of the ring. "In the challenger corner we have Mac. I don't know a thing about him other than I think he's gonna be dead meat in a couple of minutes."

Laughter, boos and catcalls pierced the crowd. It was pretty obvious to Mac that he was the outsider and most if not all were going to root for Bubba.

"In the champion's corner we have our own Bubba the Barbarian." yelled the announcer.

"Woe." said Mac. As the cheers and cries echo in the large hall. "I may be in trouble here."

"Fighters come to the center of the ring. I'd tell you the rules but there are none. I'd have you shake hands but Bubba can't stand your guts. So all I have to say is, once I'm out of the way, fight until Mac is unconscious. Have at em Bubba."

Before Mac realized what was happening he was being hugged like a bear and it took his breath away. Mac's mind raced back to his fight training and how Josh had taught him to get out of this very hold. Two thumbs in the eyes, a huge scream from Bubba and Mac was free. Before Bubba knew what hit him he was being pummeled with a dozen or so punches to the face and midsection.

"Man, you're fast." screamed Bubba retreating to the other side of the cage. "But now I'm mad."

Good, he'll be out of control now. I should be able to handle him if I can keep my senses. thought Mac.

Bubba charged with nostrils enlarged and face bloodied like a raging bull. With one side step and a kick in the rear he slammed into the cage fencing springing him backward. On the way down Mac whacked him in the gut as hard as he could. Again, Mac pummeled him with a dozen or more to the face and ribs. Flailing to protect himself Bubba got in a lucky shot to Mac's nose sending blood to the floor below. Stumbling backwards Mac caught himself on the cage. Rolling over and pushing himself up from the floor Bubba was just about upright when he caught a flying kick to the jaw. The fight was over and the hushed crowd was stunned.

"Way to go Mac. I knew you had it in you." said Billy. "Come on I'll buy you another beer. I can afford it. I'm the only one who bet on you and the odds were pretty good."

Chapter Twelve

"Where is he," shouted Bubba.

Mac jumped from the bar stool and prepared for an explosion as Bubba spotted him and lumbered over. In a sideward stance with his hands in his fight position Mac was taken back when Bubba stuck out his hand and with a grin on his face said,

"Good fight man. You kicked my butt far and square and no one's done that to me before. You move like greased lightning. Where'd you learn to fight like that? Billy, we gotta get this dude to join the Sons."

"Hey Bubba, I was just gettin to that, when you busted through the door. How bout it Mac, want to join the Sons of Lucifer?"

"What's it take to get in with you guys?" asked Mac.

"First thing you need is a sponsor and I'll do that."

"Come on Billy, let me be his sponsor. I'm the one he whipped up on," said Bubba.

"Why don't both of us sponsor him. That way we can run em ragged waiting on us,"chuckled Billy. "How about it Mac, you want Bubba and me to be your sponsors?"

"What's this waiting on you stuff? I've never been much of a servant."

"You've gotta be a pledge until you prove yourself worthy of the club. That means you run errands for us and fetch our beers and protect our women."

"Just remember that you keep your hands off our women," said Bubba. All you do is protect them, we do the other stuff."

"I think I'm getting to like you Bubba. Willie, give this barbarian a beer."

"Here ya go Bubba," said Willie. "Billy you wanted me to remind you when it was 4:00 pm. Its time."

"Thanks baby. I gotta head out for a couple of hours."

"Hey, Sons, Listen up for a minute," yelled Sonny. "Billy had a run in with some of the Fire Gang members earlier today. It looks like they want to pick us off one by one, so no one rides alone until we can deal with em."

"Shoot. Hey Mac, come on you get to ride with me? Looks like I need a tag-a-long and that's what pledges do."

"Sure Billy, no sweat. Where we headin?

"Where is none of your business. You just stick with me. Hey Sonny, Me and Bubba are gonna sponsor the new guy. We'll do the formalities when I get back. I gotta run and he's riding with me."

"Yeah, okay," yelled Sonny waving his hand as he walked into the back room. "Keep an eye out for those a-holes."

As Mac looked at the gray mass of clouds looming over the Southern horizon he knew it would a matter of minutes before they were running in the rain. What should have taken thirty minutes took forty as they faced one downpour after another. Billy finally pulled into a strip mall and parked in front of

Mid-West Floral. As they got off the bikes billy spoke up.

"You stay here with the bikes."

Mac, soaked to the bone, was glad the rain let up as he did his best to dry off. Billy walked out of the store and strapped a bundled of flowers, wrapped in heavy plastic, to the back of his seat. And shouted, "Let's ride."

What in blazes is he going to do with those flowers? I thought Willie was his woman. Man, I hope I don't have to cover for him.

About ten minutes out the sun squinted through the clouds and the threat of more rain disappeared as the skies cleared. Mac was starting to get worried as they headed into Lake Haven. He had been a pastor in the area for 15 years. A lot of people knew him and even with his new look someone might recognize him. Relief came as they headed straight through town. Just when he was beginning to relax Billy turned into the county cemetery and pulled up to the section that Pam was buried in.

What in the world is going on? What is this dude doing?

Unwrapping the flowers Billy looked at Mac and said, "You stay here pledge, I'll be right back."

Mac watched, with a burning sense of anger swelling up inside of him, as Billy walked over to Pam's grave and took the old flowers out and placed the beautiful new ones into the urn.

"Hey, Pastor. I haven't seen you around for quite some time," yelled the grounds keeper.

Mac jumped off of his bike and made a quick move up the road to the young man.

"Play along or we're both dead," whispered Mac as he tucked a hundred dollar bill into the young man's hand.

Billy ran up to them with his hand on the handle of the revolver he kept in his back belt.

"You know this guy, Mac?"

I sure as hell do" as he grabbed him by the shirt collar. "He owes me a hundred bucks from some pot I sold him a couple weeks ago. You got my money?"

"Um. Yeah, that's why I yelled to you. Here, one hundred smackers. Have you got any more weed? That was some good smoke you sold me."

"Naw, my supplier got busted. Go on get outta here. We're busy."

"Sorry about that Billy. Didn't mean to interrupt you. Who's in that grave?"

"Come on, I'll tell you about it. You tell anyone else we've been anywhere near here and I swear I will blow your frigging head off. By the way, what'd that dude call you?"

"What did he call me? I don't know I just heard him yell."

It took everything Mac had not to break down as they walked up to Pam's headstone. Her memory filled his mind as he pictured her lovely face. He missed her so much.

"Who is this Pam McIntyre to you Billy?

"Remember that woman who was beat to death in Lake Haven last summer?"

"Yeah, I remember reading something about that. Is this her?"

"Have you noticed that dent on my gas tank?"

"Yeah."

"It was my bike that she hit and knocked over. By the time I got out of the store, Bubba and three other Sons had beat her so bad. Man, it was awful. I couldn't stop them in time. They just kept beating her." A tear trickled down his face as he turned, bent down and fluffed the flowers. "I come once a week and put flowers on her grave."

Pastor Mike reached into his jacket and pulled out his 38.

Chapter Thirteen

Mac felt the tears running down his cheeks. Wiping it away with his gun hand he suddenly realized that now was not the time to exact his revenge. Billy turned around just as mac quietly slipped his 38 back into his jacket.

"Listen pledge, you let any one know about what I do here you will be sorry. Got that."

"I got that," said Mac as he quickly turned and walked towards his bike hiding his tears. "You ready to get out of here. I'd like to get out of these wet clothes, my crotch is starting to itch."

"Yeah, let's roll. There's a bar and grill up the road I'll buy dinner, you buy the beer. We can dry out as we eat."

I've lived here for 15 years. I wonder why I never saw this dive before. You would've thought I would notice the big flashing sign advertising Bert's Bar and Grill. I guess not a lot of our church people visited here. No one should recognize me in this place. I'll just be another biker dude fitting into the woodwork.

"So that lady hit your bike and you beat her to death?" said Mac chomping down on his burger.

"No, I was in the store when she did it. Bubba and the guys lost it. It's just a bike. I may be bad to the bone but I wouldn't hit a woman over a machine. Especially one that good lookin. I leave the dent to remind me of what happened that day."

"Who were the guys with Bubba?"

"Asking a lot of questions dude. Some things are better left unsaid."

"Hey man, it looked like you wanted to vent a little bit so I'm just givin you a chance to talk about it."

"I don't know you very well yet, but you don't strike me as a shrink."

"That'll be the day. I might be a little crazy but not that crazy," laughed Mac. "Seriously, if you want to get it off your chest I'm here to listen. It'll go no further than you and me and these four walls."

Mac's mind raced back to the days of his counseling ministry as a pastor. He would often give folks the assurance they could spill their guts to him and he would keep it confidential with those very words. This time his goal was to find out who else was involved in Pam's murder.

"I appreciate that. It's hard to find someone that can be trusted to keep their mouth shut. Buy me another Bud and I'll tell you the story. And remember that I'll get even if you tell anyone that I have this soft side in me.

"Here ya go, one Bud in the long neck. So what went down with this lady."

"Thanks man. We had just parked in front of the book store on Jackson street in Lake Haven. I wanted to pick up a new biker magazine, so I went into the store. Bubba, his prospect Mikey, Slim Jim and the Mouth, were out front goofing off when Pam McIntyre tried to parallel park and backed into my bike. She got out and apologized profusely to the guys. The Mouth made some nasty comment to her and she started to cry. Mikey got bent out of shape and pushed her into Bubba's arms and he gave her a kiss and manhandled her. She slapped him and he hit her and they just started to beat her senseless. By the time I got out of the store it was all over. Mikey grabbed her wallet and we split."

"Who's the Mouth?"

"He's the little mouthy guy doing the announcements in the fight cage. He used to be a radio D.J. Before they canned him. He's as squirrely as he looks. My phones buzzing, I gotta take this."

That was hard to sit and listen too. Thought Mac. *At least Billy had nothing to do with Pam's death. Man, I almost took my revenge on the wrong guy.*

"That was Willie. We gotta go, somethings gone down at the complex."

* * * * *

A block away from the complex, Billy pointed to a lone figure on the rooftop of the old, abandoned, Eastside Hotel. Mac could make out a rifle with scope pointed in the direction they had just ridden. As they parked their bikes he pointed to the West corner of their warehouse building to another leather clad lookout scanning the horizon with binoculars.

"What gives?" questioned Mac

"It looks like something happened that brought us to condition red."

The large bar was heaped full of weapons as the Sons armed themselves with every firearm available. Billy walked over and picked up a 9mm glock pistol from the pile along with two fully loaded clips. He motioned to Mac, "Grab a gun and extra ammo. I'm gonna talk with Sonny and find out what's up."

Bubba nursed his Bud as he sat with what looked like a tear in his eye. Mac took a seat across the table as he checked the Beretta 45 for a full load.

"What's up big boy? Why the sad look," asked Mac.

"I sent Mikey across the street to get me a pizza and they gunned him down." Banging his fist on the table, "I'll kill those suckers."

"Who did it?"

"It was a couple dudes from the Fire Gang. Those dudes you and Billy tangled with earlier. Retaliation."

"Hey man, I'm sorry about Mikey. I heard you were his sponsor."

That's one I don't need to worry about. I wonder if it was God taking care of him or I'm just lucky. Either way I only have 3 more to deal with. Bubba, the Mouth and Slim Jim whoever that is. Thought Mac.

"So what do you think Bubba, we gonna go after these guys or what?"

"You bet we are. This Fire gang has just burned themselves. They aren't a match for us. We're too strong. We'll light them up in no time."

Sonny and Billy, along with 4 others, walked out of the conference room and mounted the stage on the East wall. Walking up to the front center, Sonny grabbed the microphone.

"Listen up. Willie just called from the hospital. Mikey didn't make it."

The table flew across the room and shattered when it hit the wall. Bubba's scream was heard throughout Cincinnati at the news of his friends death.

"We're sorry Bubba. We'll pay them back a hundred fold. No one messes with the Sons and gets away with it. Their heads will roll and I mean literally," as he garnished a 2 foot machete.

The whole place erupted into cheers as plans were laid out for the revenge. The hair on Mac's neck stood up as he imagined the chaos that would follow. These guys aren't messing around. An all out gang war was starting and he found himself right smack in the middle.

"Bubba, Mac, Mouth, Slim Jim. Come on over. We've got some planning to do. I'll fill you in on the details," said Billy. "Mac, you know Bubba and the Mouth from the cage, this skinny guy here is Slim Jim."

Slim was not so slim weighing more than three hundred pounds. Pure lard with hair down to his shoulders and a beard to match. Mac walked to the other side of the table to escape the smell emanating from the big man.

"Hey" said Mac, sticking out his hand.

Now that I know who I need to get even with, my plan is coming together better than expected. You three yahoo's are the ones who are going to lose their heads.

"Okay, listen up. This is going to be an all out war. Some of us are going to get injured. We need to get some meds so our ladies can patch us up. We're going to take down the Fargo Pharmacy over on Sixth Street tomorrow night. Mac, you and I are going to be the lookouts. I'll man the back door and you'll be around the corner watching the front and side street. Mouth, since you're the smallest, will go in through the window behind the dumpster and open the back door for Bubba and Slim. It ought to be a simple job. In and out in a matter of minutes. Slim you grab all the gauze, bandages and tape you can carry in your backpack. Bubba, you and Mouth jump the counter and find all the pain killers and antibiotics you can find and anything else that might be helpful. Okay, it's getting late so you all go get some rest and watch your backs. Meet me back here at 10:00 sharp tomorrow morning."

"That's my phone," said Mac. "Hello."

"Pastor McIntyre, this is Detective Jim Oakes," whispered the detective.

"It's my mom. Okay if I take this. My dad has been pretty sick the last few months."

"Yeah, no sweat. We're heading out anyways."

"I'm right in the middle of something. Can I call you later?" Mac said as he walked away from the table.

"I know you're with the Sons. We've gotta talk. Can you get away and meet me."

"Yeah, I was just leaving. Do you know where my place is over on 8th Street?"

"yeah, its the old West side garage."

"Okay I'll see you in about half hour."

"Hey Billy." Mac said as he flipped his phone shut. "I have to go see my dad. Doesn't look like he's gonna make it much longer. My mom's flippin out."

"Okay. Be here at 10:00 A.M. sharp no matter what. Stay alert for those fire dudes."

Chapter Fourteen

"Who's the new guy?" Susan shouted as she pointed at the video of Billy and Mac pulling up to the complex. "Where'd he come from? Come on people give me some information on him"

Susan Coffey, special agent of the FBI and head of the Midwest organized crime task force, was all business as she attempted to shut down the Sons of Lucifer. For the last two years all the auburn haired beauty's time had been wrapped up in trying to infiltrate and document the goings and comings of the Sons. They allowed no one new to enter their clubhouse and it was impossible to get an undercover operative any where close to the gang.

Police officers, detectives and FBI agents gathered around the video to get a better look at the individual who seemed to just appear out of nowhere.

"All we know about him is that he helped Billy out at the bank this morning. He's a pretty good fighter and he shot one of the Fire Gang members in the leg in order to get Billy out of a jam," said a surveillance agent.

"Has anyone run his license plate?"

"We have, but it doesn't show up in any records. We got his fingerprints from a little diner he ate at right before the fight, but they're not in any federal or state files. We have no idea who he is."

"Can you use some software to remove the facial growth and shorten the hair? This guy looks familiar to me. I just can't place him," said Detective Jim Oakes, from Lake Haven.

"Jaydon, you got the equipment to do that?" Susan asked.

"Yeah, no problem but it'll take me a minute to clip the picture from the video into the software."

Agent Jaydon began trimming the hair and removing the mustache and beard from the face on the screen.

"Oh man, that's Pastor Mike McIntyre. He's the reason I joined the task force to begin with. They murdered his wife a few months back and I couldn't prove a thing. I figured this was my best bet to lock them up. There's only one reason that he's involved. Revenge!"

"Then, he's our man on the inside," stated Susan

"No way. This guy's a pastor. He's no match for these outlaws. They'll eat him alive. We've gotta get him outta there."

"Not gonna happen. We've been trying for two years to get someone into their gang. This guy's in and he is staying in. Oakes, you contact him and arrange a meeting. These guys are going down once and for all."

"I'll do my best. However, I can guarantee he won't work with you. Maybe I can plant a bug on him. Have you got anything small that I can stick on his jacket."

"Jaydon, make it happen," commanded Susan.

* * * * *

"It's all set. I'm gonna meet him in half an hour. You got that bug for me, Jaydon?"

"Sure do. Come over here and let me show you how it works.

As Detective Oakes walked over, Agent Jaydon quickly reached up and straightened the man's collar.

"So let me see this little thing."

"Take a look under your lapel, Jim."

"Huh. Man, you are good at what you do."

"Okay. See this little rubber antenna? You just slip it through your fingers like so. Then you can hide it on the inside of your hand like this. It's got this sticky glue on this side and all you have to do is get it under his jacket collar. It'll be up to you to figure out how to get that close to his jacket."

"Oakes, take a couple of agents with you," commanded Susan. "Get this guy on our side."

"No way. It'll be better if I see him alone. I think he trusts me. I gotta go. I'm meeting him over on the West side."

Chapter Fifteen

Mac parked his bike in the garage bay at his shop. Walking into the store front he flipped on the lights and plopped into his chair, kicked his feet up on the desk and waited for Detective Oakes to arrive. He was startled awake by the rapping on the window.

"Hey detective, come on in. What can I do for you?"

"Let's move into the back just in case someone rides by and sees us talking," said Oakes.

Mac flipped off the lights as they made their way into the corner he had set up for fight training.

"Looks like you've been working out. I noticed your motorcycle looks as mean as you do. What do you think you're trying to do getting involved with the Sons? Man, they're way out of your league. Let us handle them."

"You said yourself that you couldn't prove a thing. I'm gonna get even if it is the last thing I do. They took the love of my life away from me and I can't forget that."

"Listen, pastor, we have a task force watching the gang and we need an inside man," said Oakes as he grab Mac by the collar and quickly stuck the bug under his lapel. "You need to help us. I don't know how you got in with them so easily but you've been able to do what we haven't. All we need is some proof and we can put them away for a long time."

"No way, detective. It is not gonna happen. I don't want them in prison. I want them dead," pushing away Oakes' hands. "Feel free to leave at any time."

"Come on, don't do anything stupid. You'll end up in prison or worse."

"Listen detective, I'm not going to help you guys bust these dudes for some racketeering charge. My mind is made up and you need to go."

"I'll leave, but you be careful. These guys don't play games."

Mac locked the door as the detective walked out and hit the sack.

* * * * *

Mac walked into the Sons of Lucifer's complex at 9:55 A.M. ready for the final instructions for the break-in later that night. Bubba, Mouth and Slim Jim sat at a table at the far end of the room each nursing a beer.

"You guys drinking breakfast today," questioned Mac as he pulled up a chair.

"We been here all night thinking about Mikey and those idiot who gunned him down," said Bubba.

"You better be wide awake for tonight," said Billy suddenly appearing and sitting down. "Let's go over this one more time. Mac and I will be the lookouts. I'll be at the back door and he'll be watching the front and side streets. Mouth will go in through the back window behind the dumpster and open the back door for bubba and Slim Jim. Slim, you grab as much gauze and bandages as you can carry while Bubba and Mouth are grabbing the meds.

Simple in and out, under three minutes. Any questions?"

"What time are we hitting this place and where do we meet up," questioned Slim Jim.

"We'll head out from here at 10:30 P.M. and head over to Fargo's about 11:00. Don't be late we'll want to check the place out for a few minutes before we knock it over. Okay, you three go get some sleep and be ready for tonight."

Yeah, I could use a little shut eye," said the Mouth. "Come on Bubba, Slim let's get outta here."

"Mac, how's your old man doing?"

"Better than I thought. My mom gets a little over excited when it comes to him. They've been together over 50 years. Thanks for asking."

"How about you are your parents around?"

"Naw, they died when I was like three. Don't remember them at all. I was kicked around from foster home to foster home. I was a little handful. The last ones were okay. They got me into college and talked me into getting my MBA. I think they were hoping to get me out of the biker life. I was already riding with Sonny and the boys. In fact he made sure my college bills were paid. I think he wanted someone with some smarts to help him run this group of misfits. Anyway, I still stop by and see them. I guess they're the closest thing I have to family outside of the Sons."

"Wow, sounds like an interesting life. What are your plans for the rest of today?"

"I gotta take Willie to work in about ten minutes. Want to ride along?"

"Sure why not. Then we can stop and get some lunch. That dinner by the bank we met at serves a great sandwich."

"Works for me. Hey Willie, you ready to ride," Billy called out.

* * * * *

"You know this place is only a couple of blocks from the Fire Gang hangout, don't you?"

"No Billy, I never really thought about that when I picked it."

"No matter, the food was worth the risk. That's one of the best Rueben's I've had in a long time. I'm gonna head home and get some sleep before the job tonight. I would suggest you do the same. It'll be a long night. "

Okay, I'll see you around 10:30 then. Ride safe and watch your backside."

Chapter Sixteen

"Who put that box there," questioned Mac as he pulled up to his garage door.

Dear Pastor McIntyre,

When we were moving into our new home we found this box of stuff left in the basement. Not knowing if you meant to leave it here or not we rummaged through it. It looks like most of the stuff was your wife's things so we thought you might want it.

We tried to call a number of times, but could not get an answer. We asked Sally, our real estate agent, if she knew where you lived. She gave us this address. We hope this is the correct place and you get these things.

If whoever is reading this is not Mike McIntyre and you do not know him or where he can be found, please discard these items.

Sincerely Yours,

Sam and Beth Harvey

Oh, great! Now I'll have to go through this stuff all over again. Why didn't they just dump it all?
Mac set the box down next to his front desk and flopped into his chair. He flipped the box open.

First he pulled out Pam's favorite photo. They were enjoying a fellowship at the church when someone told them to scrunch close for a picture. Mac had thrown his arm around Pam. His eyes were focused on the love-of-his life when the picture was snapped. His eyes were filled with tears as he focused on her. She had been taken from him way too early in such a brutal way.

Setting the picture on his desk, he reached in again and pulled out Pam's Bible. He remembered buying it less than a year before she died. The ragged edges testified of her passion for God's Word. Kicking his feet up on the desk, Mac leaned back and opened the Bible for the first time since the day that changed his life forever.

The Book fell open to one of Pam's favorite passages, Ephesians 4:30-32. In the margin Pam had Scrawled, *"Thank you Lord that the man I love, believes and lives these verses."*

Mac read the verses out loud, "And do not grieve the Holy Spirit of God, by whom you were sealed for the day of redemption. Let all bitterness, wrath, anger, clamor, and evil speaking be put away from you, with all malice. And be kind to one another, tenderhearted, forgiving one another, even as God in Christ forgave you."

"I don't want to do that! I want them to pay for what they did to Pam and me. They don't deserve my forgiveness. I'm not gonna do it," cried Mac throwing the Bible on the desk in disgust.

Pushing himself away from the desk he stormed over to the punching bag. He delivered blow after blow to the bag trying to clear his head of God's

Word. Finally, with bloody knuckles, he grabbed the bag and slid down to the floor in brokenness and tears.

"Okay, Lord You win. I have been wrong all these months trying to get revenge. I know that you say, 'vengeance is mine.' I'll leave it in your hands even though I am so close to getting even."

As Mac walked out the door of his shop he knew what had to be done. Throwing gravel as he sped out onto the road his mind flashed back to the words he had used in counseling a young man just days before Pam's murder.

"Sam, I know it's been hard on you. The things those people said and did to you were unjustified. They were flat out wrong to treat you like that. However, if you continue to let this bitterness eat at you it'll tear you apart. God's Word tells us that we need to forgive as He forgave us. You've tried to share with them the hurt they did to you, but they refuse to deal with it. You've done your part in trying to reconcile. Now you need to move on in your walk with the Lord. The only way you can do that is to forgive them. Let God do the work in their lives from this point forward."

After fifteen minutes on the road, he knew how he would tell Billy who he was and why he was involved with the gang. Pulling up at the Son's complex he noticed most of the bikes were gone. The inside was not any different, almost a ghost town.

"Willie, I'm looking for your man. Is he around?"

"No. But, I thought you were supposed to be with him tonight?"

"Oh man. I forgot about the job. I gotta go."

As he jumped on his bike, he reflected on the plans they had made to break into the pharmacy. Rounding a corner three blocks up the road he slammed on his brakes to avoid hitting a road block.

Suddenly, Detective Jim Oakes grabbed him!

"Hold on Pastor Mike. I need you to come with me."

"I can't do that, detective. I've gotta stop something before it is too late."

"If you're talking about the pharmacy break-in that's all covered. Those guys are going down. If I know Bubba and the rest of them, they'll be going down in a blaze of gunfire."

"How did you find out about the pharmacy?"

"I put a bug on your jacket the last time we met. Pull your bike over here, you're done with this mess."

Pulling his bike around as instructed he popped the clutch and sped out. Dragging the detective to the ground.

"Son of a . . .! Get him," yelled Oakes to the troopers still at the road block.

Mac was out of sight before the troopers could get their cars turned around. Detective Oakes jumped into his car and sped off toward the pharmacy. Knowing the robbery was going down at this very minute and the pastor was on his way there, he felt rotten. He couldn't prove Billy, Bubba, Slim Jim, Mouth and Mikey had beaten Pam McIntyre to death. But now, he needed to protect Pastor McIntyre from disaster.

With the pharmacy only a mile and a half away, Mac was there in less than five minutes. He Jumped off his bike and looked around for any sign of the cops, and then headed toward the back door.

"Billy, Billy,"whispered Mac.

"Hey man, over here. Where have you been? I was beginning to think you bailed on us."

"Listen Billy, we need to get outta here. The cops'll be here any minute."

"What, how'd they find out," asked Billy as he grabbed Mac by the collar.

"Doesn't matter, we gotta get. Where are the other guys?"

"They're inside. Come on."

Creeping up to the broken window behind the dumpster, Billy called out in a hushed yell, "Bubba, we gotta go the cops are comin"

Bubba, Slim Jim and the Mouth broke through the back door and headed toward their bikes. Instantly, floodlights cut through the cover of darkness. Wafting through the burst of light was a commanding voice. "This is the police. Stop where you are. You are surrounded. Put down your weapons and get down on your knees."

Bubba and the Mouth open fire in the direction of the lights. Slim continued racing toward his bike.

"Rap, rap, rap" fills the air as the cops return fire.

"I'm hit" wails Bubba as the bullets tear through his body like a spoon through jello.

A split second later, a shot to the head lays the Mouth in a pile of his own blood. Slim Jim reached his motorcycle before he takes a bullet to the heart by a lone sniper.

"Billy, give yourself up," pleaded Mac still frozen behind the dumpster. "Don't fight it out. You can't win."

"What about you. You gonna give yourself up?"

"They know I wasn't involved. I've gotta square things with you Billy. There's no time now. Just give yourself up."

"You rat. I can't believe I trusted you."

"Man, you gotta believe me. I didn't give it up."

"I am outta here," cried Billy, as he raised his gun and headed toward his ride.

"Put your gun down or we will shoot," commanded the voice once again.

"No way I'm going to prison."

Mac jumped out from behind the dumpster and tackled Billy. The gun went off and the police opened fire. Mac positioned himself between the cops and Billy. The killing shots meant for the VP of the Sons of Lucifer, hit Pastor Mike McIntyre, mortally wounding him and sending him into the lap of his new found friend.

"Why in hell would you do that," screamed Billy

Detective Oakes rushed to the pastor's side. Doing his best to stop the bleeding he asked Pastor Mike, "Why would you save the guy who murdered your wife? You spent all these months trying to pay him back for what this low life did and you take the bullet meant for him. It doesn't make sense Pastor."

"Murdered his wife? What are you talking about?"

"Why Pastor Mike," questioned Oakes.

"I was wrong. I knew better than to get revenge. That's not my job its God's. God reminded me that I'm to love and forgive." gasped Mike clutching the detective's arm. "Oakes, Billy had nothing to do with Pam's murder. He tried to stop those other guys. Don't charge him with her death. He didn't do i . . ."

"What was he talking about? What are you talking about? Killed his wife? Who was his wife? What's the deal," questioned Billy.

"Mac is Pam McIntrye's husband? You and your buddies beat her to death last summer. He was looking to get revenge and apparently changed his mind. Why I have no idea."

"Hey man! I didn't kill her. These three idiots did that before I could stop them. I don't get it. Mac could have killed me a couple of times. Why didn't he?"

"Looks like we'll never know the answer to that question, he's gone and you're under arrest."

Chapter Seventeen

Three days had passed when Detective Jim Oakes walked into The Gospel Chapel. It had been at least fifteen years since he had been in any kind of church and he was not all that comfortable thinking he would be stuck here for a couple of hours. He usually skipped funerals for this very reason. As he scanned the surroundings he was surprised when he saw a familiar face in the crowd.

"How did you get out of jail?"

"Hey detective how goes it," quipped Billy Collins. "Our little auburn beauty, over there, got me out. I had to be at the funeral of the guy who took my place."

"Outta my way I've got to talk to Agent Coffey," said Oakes as he pushed past Billy. "Coffey, what in the . . ." He suddenly stopped when he remembered where he was. "Um, what gives? Why is Collins out? He should be put away for life."

"Calm down detective. We were able to cut a deal with him," she said softly as she pulled Oakes to a quiet corner. "He's gonna roll over on his gang. This is the first opportunity to put the majority of them away."

"No way! What'd you have to give him to do that?"

"For starters he got to come to Mac's funeral. Then we'll protect him and Willie until he testifies. Then they'll be relocated under witness protection to some God forsaken place up in the North East.

They're getting started let's find a seat it's pretty packed."

Rev. John Breckenridge opened with a prayer followed by the eulogy for Pastor Mike "Mac" McIntyre.

"I have known Mike McIntyre for almost 20 years. He served as my associate pastor for four years and then moved up here to the Gospel Chapel for the past 15 years. He loved the Lord. He and Pam were a fantastic ministry team. God used them in a mighty way in many lives. Including mine," he paused as he wiped away the tears streaming down his cheeks. "You'll have to excuse me, I will probably get choked up as I preach this morning. The McIntryes were dear friends of mine and this is tough."

The pastor continued for over 30 minutes sharing story after story of Pam and Mike's escapades as pastor and wife. The entire eulogy was very fitting for the man of God that Mike had grown into.

"Unfortunately," the pastor continued with sadness. "Mike lost his way for a short time as he dealt with the loss of his lovely wife. He got it in his mind that those who had perpetrated this tragedy had to pay. It became his own personal vengeance. He went to great lengths to exact revenge. However, and this is where it gets exciting folks, the Lord helped him to see the wrong. On his death bed Mike told detective Oakes, 'I was wrong. I knew better than to get revenge. That's not my job its God's. God reminded me that I'm to love and forgive.' That reminds me of Romans 5:6-8. Listen as I read it;

"For when we were still without strength, in due time Christ died for the ungodly. For scarcely for a righteous man will one die; yet perhaps for a good man someone would even dare to die. But God demonstrates His own love toward us, in that while we were still sinners, Christ died for us."

Folks, I don't know about you, but as I look at the end of Mike McIntyre's life, I see a man who was willing to emulate Jesus Christ. Mike died for the very man whose motorcycle Pam ran into. The accident that started this whole ball rolling. Do you get that! Mike didn't die for a righteous man. Or a good man. He died for a sinner who had a direct involvement in his wife's brutal murder. He willingly put himself in the line of fire to save someone who did not deserve to live," Breckenridge paused for affect. "Jesus Christ died for you and you do not deserve it. That's why Mike was able to die for this man. It was because of what Christ did for Him. Let me close with a question that every one of you need to consider and answer for yourself. Have you trusted Jesus Christ alone for your Lord and Savior? Let's pray."

"Wow! That was some message," Exclaimed Billy. "Oakes you gonna stay for lunch? I'd like to get your thoughts on what the pastor said."
"Nope. I'm still on the clock."

"Come on man. Even cops gotta eat. This is a free meal. They might even have a couple of donuts for ya."

"Okay, I'll stay. But no more wise cracks about donuts. Susan, I figure you don't have a choice. You gotta stay with this guy to protect your asset."

The three got their meals and found a table off in the corner. Billy asked the question. "What do you guys think about Jesus giving His life for ours?"

"Sorry, Billy, my phone's vibrating." said Oakes as he pushed himself up from the table. "I've got to get this. It's my partner. Hey Sam what's up? I told you I was gonna be at this funeral."

When Detective Oakes returned to the table he quickly grabbed his plate and alarmingly said, "I gotta go. There's been a mass murder over at the Lake Haven Golf Course. It looks like it's gonna be a long night."

The second book of the Lake Haven Murder series is a work in progress. The book ***Golf Course Massacres*** will be released in mid November 2012. Leave your email at www.concerninglife.org and we will keep you up to date on the progress.

Other fiction work by Dennis Snyder:
Road Rage vs. Forgiveness A short story

Non-Fiction work by Dr. Dennis Snyder:
The Importance of Prayer

Made in the USA
Charleston, SC
23 October 2012